CRADLE EARTH

ANDY COOMBS
SARAH SCHO

For information about licensing, translation and media rights and permission to reproduce selections from this book: Richard Flower, permissions@kidoo.com

For rights within Asia contact Eric Yang at RHK, Seoul, S.Korea.

Book design by Alisson Stasiak

Illustrations and cover art by Sarah Schofield

Edited by Thalia Mora

Kidoo Media Inc
USA: Chicago, Illinois

I never wanted it to happen. I didn't ask to become the most hunted man in British history. The papers call me a monster. The news claims I am a traitor to every human being on Earth. My friends don't answer my calls. My parents won't reply to my texts. That's why I'm leaving. I'm getting out of here.

I'm leaving you, all of you, behind.

Index

I

Dr. Erwin Katz

My name is Erwin Katz. Dr. Erwin Katz. A few months ago, I was the young star history professor at the University of London. Hundreds of people came to hear me speak every day and my classes were full of the brightest and best students from all over the world.

I specialize in the beginnings of human life. Specifically, I study evidence of the first people to live in Europe. Humans like us first came to Europe from Africa about 40,000 thousand years ago. But when they arrived, there was already a human species living here – the Neanderthals. They had lived in Europe for about 480,000 years before we arrived. Imagine that for a moment – half a million years before we arrived!

You've seen the models in museums – short people with lots of wild hair, big ridges over their eyes and thick arms and legs. You've probably seen them holding stones and cutting up meat. Wild cavemen – alien to us, but close enough for us to see ourselves in them. They are what we imagine we would have been thousands of years ago. Primitive. Dangerous. Animals.

Recently though, historians like me have found new evidence about them. We study fragments of bone. We rebuild them. We

have found proof that they painted pictures and decorated their own bodies with art. We have found out that they could talk – and from studying parts of skulls, we now know their brains were bigger than ours.

But they are not us. That's important to remember. We didn't evolve from them – we are an entirely different species. We lived at the same time as them. Yes, they came before us, but when we moved into Europe, they were here. And we lived together for about 8,000 years. And then, suddenly, about 30,000 years ago, they disappeared. They were extinct. Vanished.

There's been lots of theories. Some people think that Homo Sapiens and the Neanderthals merged and became one species. But we know from genetic evidence this is wrong. Only a small fraction of our DNA comes from Neanderthals. Some people think we hunted them and killed them all off. But again, there is no evidence for this. So, for years, no one knew for sure what happened to them.

But now I do. I know the truth.

And people want to kill me for it.

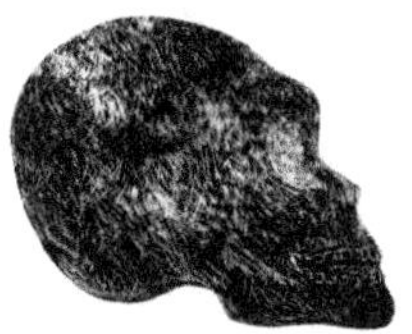

2

Old bones and stuff

Three months ago, my cell rang. It was a number I didn't recognize.

"Dr Katz speaking."

"Uh, hi. Is that Erwin?" It was a woman's voice.

"Yes, this is Erwin Katz."

"I don't know if you remember me. I'm Hilary Marsh."

I had to think for a moment. Then I remembered. I went to school years ago with Hilary Marsh. St Joseph's High. I never really knew her. We shared a couple of classes, but she was in a different group to me.

"I remember you Hilary. How can I help?"

"I saw you interviewed last year, and you were talking about old bones and stuff."

I sighed. I can't believe the way people see my work. *"That's very possible. I often do TV interviews."*

"Yeah, right. You're a bit of a star now."

She said that like she wasn't happy about it. I remembered more about Hilary. She was always a bit loud at school. Always laughing at something and tossing her hair around. She had no time for me then. How times change.

"Yes, I guess I am. But why are you calling?"

"I didn't know who else to call. I found some bones on my farm. Out in the field. I think they're human."

"Well, I don't think I am the right person to help you. You should call the police."

"I thought of that. But these bones are weird. The skull is too big."

"People have different sized heads, Hilary. I think you should call the police."

"But what if it's one of those cavemen you people are always talking about. That would be worth money, wouldn't it?"

"I suppose it would. But really, just call the…"

"Hold on. I'm sending you a picture to your phone. If you think it's nothing, then I'll go to the police."

My cell vibrated.

As the picture came in, I felt the hair on the back of my neck stand up. The skull was clearly not human. The eyebrow ridges were pronounced. The jawbone was heavy. It looked Neanderthal. And it was in perfect condition. To find a whole Neanderthal skull, unbroken, was unbelievable.

I kept my voice steady. *"I got your picture Hilary and I think you may be right. This could be something interesting. Where did you find the skull?"*

"The skull?" She said. *"It's not just the skull. Look, I'm standing over it now. I'll send you another picture."*

As the picture came through, I had to stop myself from jumping up and down. The photo was of a complete skeleton of what looked to be Neanderthalensis.

"OK. I'm coming to see you. Immediately. Send me your address and I'll be on my way."

***

I arrived at Hilary's farm just after sunset. I jumped out of the car and grabbed my field bag from the trunk. I take that bag everywhere. It has some tools, plastic gloves, brushes… everything I need to do archaeology work.

Hilary answered the door. *"That was quick."*

She hadn't changed much. She was fifteen years older, but she had the same blond hair tied up behind her head.

"Do you want a drink of something?"

"Actually, if you don't mind, I'd like to see the skeleton. Of course, I can't be sure what it is until I get a closer look."

Hilary led me around her house to the back. There were a couple of barns and chicken houses. She saw me looking around.

"They're all empty now. This was my parents' old place. I moved in here just a month ago when my divorce came through. I wanted to get my head together."

"I'm sorry," I said. But I wasn't. I was thinking about the bones lying out there somewhere.

"Just over here." Hilary shone her torch over a fence and into a field of red tulips. I jumped over the fence. I landed in mud that squelched into my shoes.

I got to my knees. The skeleton was lying on the mud. The bones were brown. I brushed at the earth around the skull. It was definitely Neanderthal. And it was perfect! But how? Neanderthal remains are over 30,000 years old. They are found buried in caves or sunk deep into earth. They are found in bits and pieces. They don't just lie in tulip fields. They are never complete.

"So, you were digging in the field and you found this?" I asked.

"No. I got up this morning and when I came out, here it was. We had rain last night. Perhaps the water washed it up."

This was impossible. Maybe someone was playing a trick on me. I touched the bone of the arm and felt the ribs. It was real. I was sure of it. I've studied and researched hundreds of Neanderthal remains… nothing like this, but I know what is real and what is not. This was. But how could it be here? Like this?

"Is there somewhere I can put the skeleton tonight? I will need to study it here. I am afraid if I try to get to my university it may break."

"You can use one of the barns. I'll show you."

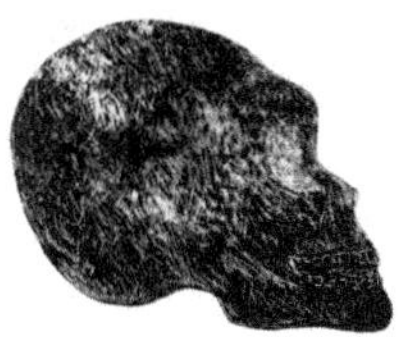

3

The skeleton

I was lying in Hilary's spare room looking at the ceiling. Dawn was just coming up. I hadn't slept. It had taken me two hours to move the bones into the barn.

There was an old table that I had carefully put the skeleton on. Piece by piece, I rearranged it to make it whole once again. I used my brushes and distilled water to gently remove the mud and earth. When I had finished, seven hours later, the Neanderthal skeleton lay on the table, white and fresh. It looked new. The bones were not scratched. There were no breaks.

I had unpacked my equipment from the car and scratched a tiny bone sample into a test-tube from the top of the skull for analysis. There was no doubt in my mind that this was real. Hilary Marsh had found maybe the most important archaeological discovery for a hundred years simply lying in her field. And she had called me. Thank you, Hilary. Thank you, St Joseph's!

I opened my eyes an hour later. I was still in my clothes from the day before. I ran downstairs. Hilary was up and making coffee. The TV was on.

"Do you want a cup?" she asked.

"Yes. White. Three sugars, please."

"Sweet tooth, eh?"

"Yes."

"I don't remember you being so sweet," she said.

I blushed. Hilary Marsh had just called me sweet. If that had happened when I was at school, it would have been the biggest thing ever. But now, here I was, a grown man, respected historian, blushing red at a compliment. I shook it off.

"I always was. You just never noticed."

"Oh, I'm sure that's not right," she said, coming over and handing me a cup. *"I was just too shy to say anything."*

I knew that wasn't true. Hilary Marsh was the least shy person I had ever met. But the idea was nice. She started to talk about the old days at school, but a picture on the TV caught my attention.

"Hey, can we turn that up?" I said.

"…was found today in a small village south of London. The bones are from what appears to be a caveman. Our reporter has the story."

The image changed to a man standing in a park. Behind him was a lot of activity - men and women in white coats and plastic gloves.

The reporter started to speak. *"Here in this sleepy rural village the remains of a caveman or Neanderthal as scientists call it, have been found. At five a.m. this morning, Mrs. O'Doone was walking her dog when she…"*

I turned to Hilary. *"Did you tell anyone?"*

"What?" She looked at me, surprised. *"No, of course I didn't."*

I wasn't really listening. I ran outside and into the barn. My skeleton was still there. Nobody had moved it. But something had changed. Last night I had left it clean and washed. This morning the bones were covered with a kind of green mud or something. I touched it with my finger. It was damp. Damn it! Maybe it was a type of mold. I should have dried the bones before I went to bed. I went back into the house.

"There's another one!" Hilary exclaimed.

"I know. I saw," I replied curtly.

"No, I mean another one. Look. They're saying there are more. All over England."

On the TV they were showing a map of the UK. On the map were little skull icons dotted about. The presenter was pointing at the map.

"The skulls represent where a skeleton has been found. So far, we have reports of more than fifteen such skeletons being found." The presenter put his finger to his ear. *"No, sorry, twenty-two complete remains have now been reported. And as I speak more are being discovered. For more detailed analysis, we hand you over to our special science correspondent."*

On the TV the face of an old man appeared. I knew him. Professor James Harris. He used to be my teacher when I went to college.

"This is extraordinary," he said. *"To find one Neanderthal remains is amazing but so many and in such a short space of time is... unbelievable. There will be an explanation – maybe a prank or a joke by students, but how did they coordinate their activity so well all over the country? These skeletons are appearing everywhere.*

The circumstances are the same. They are not found buried but simply lying on top of the earth. Complete Neanderthal, or Homo Neanderthalensis to give the proper name. I admit, I really don't know what else to say."

Hilary switched the TV off.

"Well, that's it," she said.

"Hey, I was watching that!" I wanted to hear more.

"What else is there to watch? Loads of these things are turning up everywhere. It won't be worth much money now. We may as well call someone to take it away. At least we'll get on the TV." She took out her cell.

She wanted to call people. There was too much to find out. I had to think fast.

"Look, all those other people have reported it. The police are probably going to take the bones away. Just because they have found twenty or even thirty, doesn't mean it's not going to be worth a lot of money."

She put her cell down. *"What do you mean?"*

"Well, how many diamonds are there in the world? Thousands. Probably more. But they are still worth a lot of money. Neanderthal skeletons are much rarer. So, what if they find twenty or even fifty? It's still very valuable."

"You really think so?" Her eyes were gleaming.

"I'm sure of it. I'm the expert. Probably out of all the people in England you called the right one. Me. I know all there is to know

about Neanderthals and trust me, what you have in your barn is a gold mine. Just give me a couple of days to think about things and I will make us both… very rich.”

“The magic words,” Hilary said and clapped. *“Ok then. What do we need to do?”*

“We just play it cool. I will keep studying the bones and, in a day or so, we can plan our next move. Just trust me, ok?”

She came over and put her arms around me. *“Of course, I do. As you say, you're the expert.”* She kissed me on the cheek. *“Now, how about some breakfast?”*

“Good idea. You make us something to eat. I'll go and start work.”

As I got some water and a cloth, I breathed a sigh of relief. I needed time to figure out what was happening. Things were moving too fast. So many had been found… it was impossible! It must be a prank as my old teacher had said. But I am an expert. I know what a fake looks like. And what was lying in the barn was no fake. I was sure of it.

I went out to the barn and tried to clean the bones again. But the green stuff wouldn't come off. In fact, it looked like over the last ten minutes it had got worse. It was slimy and wet. And now it had spread to almost all the bones. I went back inside. I needed to call someone and ask them to send me some special equipment. I needed electric brushes and some chemical cleaner. I had to protect the bones.

When I got back in, Hilary was laying out plates of food. I realized I was very hungry. I sat down and started to eat. Hilary switched her screen on again. The map was back. There were now many more little skull icons. I turned back to my food. I needed to think.

I found James Harris' number in my mobile and got through to him on the second ring.

"I saw you on the news, James," I said. *"You looked worried."*

"Erwin? Is that you? Isn't this incredible! I actually got to see one up close and you know, I'm sure it's real." His voice was rushed. Excited.

"Me too." I explained to him where I was and what had happened. *"But James, don't tell anyone I'm here. I don't know what's going to happen, but I want to keep this just to us at the moment. Something is going on here, and I want to find out what. But I need your help."*

I told him what equipment I needed to help in my research and stressed that I didn't want him telling anyone where I was. I already had over a hundred missed calls on my cell. Suddenly, every news media wanted to talk to a Neanderthal expert. And I am The Expert. But I didn't want to talk to anyone. Yes, I could have made thousands of pounds for appearing on shows, but I knew something was happening here. Something more than money. Something huge.

The stuff would take a day or two to arrive. Until then there wasn't much else I could do. I didn't want to put any pressure on the bones in case I broke them. I just had to wait.

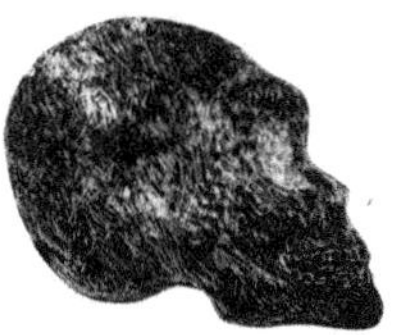

4

The mold

The next day the slimy mold had grown to completely cover the skeleton in the barn. But overnight, the bones story or the "mysterious caveman skeleton appearances" as the press had so unimaginatively called it, had taken over everything.

Hilary had the news on all the time. More and more of the skeletons had appeared and it wasn't just in England. All over the globe, from Paris to Romania, Johannesburg, Baghdad, Sydney to Cairo - skeletons had appeared and were being looked at by the authorities. The numbers were staggering. So far, about 9,000 had been reported. And it seemed as though the green slimy mold wasn't just my problem. My old friend, James Harris, was back on TV.

"Another strange thing about this, if it can get any stranger, is the mold that seems to be growing on all the bones. With the right equipment, it can be cleaned off but then it comes back again, twice as quickly. Even in completely sterile environments, the mold grows. This shouldn't happen. It's not logical. Then again, nothing about any of this is logical."

His eyes were confused. I felt sorry for my old teacher and glad that I wasn't on TV as well – trying to explain all this but ending up looking as dumb as everybody else. I wanted to wait until I had answers before I said anything public. I had my reputation to think of.

And then, things started to get really crazy. The following morning, I went out to look at the Neanderthal remains. Overnight, the mold had spread rapidly. You couldn't even see the bones anymore. And the mold had shape. In the middle of the ribs a large lump of stuff had formed. It looked like a heart. In the eye sockets a clear jelly had grown. They looked like the beginnings of eyes! I looked back at the heart lump. And, as I studied it, I became aware that I could actually see the brown slime move. Lines, like sticky worms, were moving slowly from the lump. With a jump, I realized that they were veins. All over the bones, stuff was growing and taking shape. Somehow, a body was growing onto the bones. This wasn't mold. It was flesh!

I turned and ran out. I needed to breathe. I gulped at the air. I needed to show someone… Hilary was the only person around. I ran into the farmhouse. Hilary was standing, mouth open, staring at the screen. She turned to look at me.

"Erwin?" was all she said.

It was the same on all channels. Overnight, the police had moved in and taken the bones away. All over the world. A serious looking man was talking on networks. The caption under his image identified him as a senior government minister. And next to his name, in red letters, was NATIONAL EMERGENCY.

"We ask all people not to panic. The bones of cavemen recently found all over the world are infected with a virus that may be dangerous. We ask all people who have any contact with these bones to report to their local police station for possible decontamination procedures. People who have had contact are becoming sick. It is very important that all finds are reported immediately. If you do not

report any bones you find, you may face legal action and maybe even prison. We are not sure what is happening at the moment. This may even be the work of terrorists. But do not be afraid. We have teams of people who are trained to deal with this sort of thing. You will be protected."

Hilary's face was white. *"Are we sick? Are we going to die?"*

"We are going to be fine, Hilary." I tried to keep my voice steady. *"Trust me. This is just the government's way of trying to keep control. Don't worry. We will not be arrested. Remember who I am."*

"Don't you think we should report it now? This is serious. Look at this!" She pointed to her open laptop on a coffee table. She sat down and clicked on a link. I sat down next to her.

The link took us to a blog site. There were pictures of a skeleton with the same stuff growing on it. Underneath was the caption,

"End of the World!"

The threads were full of all kinds of crazy ideas. Some people thought it was the American government trying to take over the world. Some thought that terrorists were attacking with a biological weapon. One blog that scared me the most was from a group calling themselves "The Sons of God's Anger". They had quoted bits from the bible about the end of days. They said that just before the end of the world the dead would rise from the ground. They thought that we had angered God and he was coming for us, or something like that. I closed the laptop.

"What if they are right?" Hilary stood up. *"This is scary!"*

"Yes, it is. But we shouldn't report it. Just think. If we keep low now and all the other skeletons are taken away, then we will have the only one. Just imagine what a network will pay for our story."

The money talk was winning again. But Hilary still looked worried. *"Ok. If you say so. But if we are arrested, I'm going to say that it was your idea, ok?"*

"Sure. Whatever. No problem. I take full responsibility."

"But if we do get lots of money then I want …," she narrowed her eyes in concentration, *"…eighty percent of everything, ok? I mean, that's only fair. I found it. I called you."*

"Sure, eighty percent. Sounds good."

Hilary was ok for now. But what was happening in the barn? What was happening to the world?

***

The next morning, when I looked at the Neanderthal bones, I was sure. This was no virus. That story was a cover. The government was panicking. We weren't sick and I knew that the bones were not infectious. Something much weirder was happening.

The Neanderthal remains had changed completely. The skeleton was now a body.

Muscles had grown – green and brown and red. Tendons, veins, even in places a white milky substance that could be skin was stretching and growing over the body. It was as if time were going backwards. Bodies decay to bones. But these bones were changing into a fully formed body!

As I watched, the process got faster and faster. Time seemed to speed up. I could actually see patches of skin form. The jelly-eyes turned green and pupils appeared in the middle. Then, almost immediately, skin formed over them. Eyelids! Lashes!

I could see now that this was a female. Breast tissue formed and then in five minutes was covered in a pink skin. Toes and fingers fleshed out and then nails grew from under them. It was like seeing a nature documentary of a flower grow really fast – with the sun and clouds speeding overhead. But this was no camera trick, and this was no plant. This was a Neanderthal woman!

The legs and arms grew thick and strong. And then I watched, unbelieving, as light brown hair sprouted, grass from skin, flowing over the head. Lips took shape. Teeth grew and pushed the lips to form a full mouth. The whole body was moving with the growth. Rippling, Becoming.

And then, it stopped. Stillness. The process, whatever it was, was complete. And I was looking at a Neanderthal woman lying on a table. As if she died moments ago.

Her body was like ours. But thicker and smaller. Her head was bigger and the bumps over her eyes looked strange. But she had less hair than an adult human. The hairline on her head was farther back. And her skin was very pale.

I was sitting down – looking at her. I realized I hadn't breathed properly for maybe twenty minutes or so. My head was spinning.

I took deep breaths. In and out. My nostrils flared.

I reached out my hand and touched a finger to her mouth. I pulled my finger back. Startled. The skin was not cold! My world moved. It was as if I had fallen through a dark hole into a different place. Everything I knew was upside down. And then, my world vanished in a pop and I leapt back from my chair – knocking it over. The Neanderthal had opened her eyes!

***

How do I explain this? Imagine you are looking at a rock, and the rock opens up and looks back at you. You touch an ancient shell on a faraway beach and the shell sings. Imagine that everything you have ever been taught; everything that science and common sense tells you is real, is a lie. Up is down, black is white, and you are not you. The world is not the world. Our moon is made of cheese and the stars are made of snow. That is how I felt as I looked into the eyes of this 30,000-year-old Neanderthal woman. Can you imagine? Is it possible? And then, imagine she spoke. Because she did.

The woman pushed herself up and swung her legs off the side of the table. Her legs were too short to reach the floor. She flexed her toes. She kept her eyes on mine. She frowned slightly, as though confused. I nearly laughed. She was confused! And then she opened her lips, and a sound came out. She coughed. It was such a normal thing to do that I did laugh.

And then she said, *"Sorry, I was trying to say, don't be afraid."*

I looked at her. I laughed again. My laugh was like a bark. I blinked. I tried to swallow, but my mouth was too dry. I felt cold. I shivered.

"Do you understand me?" she asked. She frowned again.

I nodded.

"Yes, you do. I can see it. But you are afraid. Please. Don't be afraid. I won't hurt you."

I looked at her – a naked woman from prehistory. I laughed again.

"I am here to talk to you. To understand. Will you talk to me?"

I nodded. I swallowed again. *"Ye… ye… yes,"* I managed.

"Good. But first I'm hungry. Do you have energy I can eat? Do you have food? Do you have water?"

"I'll… I'll… get you some," I said. I backed away.

***

In the house, Hilary was watching TV again. She didn't turn round as I ran in.

"There are soldiers everywhere," she said. *"I phoned a friend in town and the soldiers are on all the streets. There must be terrorists. People are freaking out."*

"It's not terrorists," I said woodenly.

The same government man was on TV. He was saying the same thing over the same caption: NATIONAL EMERGENCY.

"It's just a recording now," Hilary said. She looked at me. Her eyes were frightened. *"There's no new information. Just that we should contact the police if we know anything."*

"We wait," I said. *"The plan is the same."*

"Yes, but what if…"

I interrupted her. *"The plan is the same,"* I said harshly. *"Now, I'm going to get some food and go back to my work. Can you stay calm here?"*

She nodded.

I took food from the fridge and a bottle of water and went back to the barn.

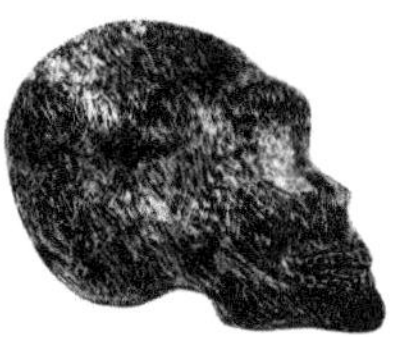

5

Pepkari

The Neanderthal woman was standing next to the table when I walked in. She was touching her face with her fingers as though exploring its shape. She was much smaller than me. I stood by the door, silently watching her as she put her hands to her hair and smoothed it down. I realized I wasn't frightened any more. Apart from the large head and wide arms and legs, she looked… normal.

"I have food," I said. *"And water."*

She looked up at me and smiled. I smiled back. She walked towards me and took the food. She started to eat. She was very hungry. For maybe a minute she ate – all concentration on the food. I opened the water and handed her the bottle. She drank half of it down in one.

"So, you know what a bottle is," I said.

"Yes. I got the picture from your mind. Simple really."

I sat down on the table where she had lain. Growing a body. *"You got the picture from my mind? Are you telepathic?"*

"Yes, of course. It's how I know your words. Your language. I find the words in your mind and I can speak them to you. My language is different. Do you want to hear?"

I nodded again.

She spoke quickly. I understood nothing. It sounded like leaves moving and a bird singing. And it was beautiful. Half song, half words. High and sweet.

"What did you say?"

"I said my name is Pepkari and it's good to meet you." She smiled again. Her teeth were big. *"Would you prefer, take me to your leader?"* She winked at me.

"My name is Erwin," I said, and held out my hand.

I immediately felt stupid and started to pull it away. I was trying to shake hands with a Neanderthal! But she took it and held it tight. Her palm was warm and dry. She even shook it up and down.

"I know. You are Dr Erwin Katz, and you are an expert in my people. A student of what you call Homo Neanderthalensis. I am lucky to have met you. But from the pictures I see in your mind your ideas of us are very wrong." She looked at me and frowned again. *"Very wrong. You need to have a better imagination. I'm sorry, is that rude?"*

I laughed again. *"No. It's not. And I think you may be right. If your people can come back from the dead and re-grow your bodies after thousands of years, then yes. Definitely. My ideas are wrong."*

Pepkari took another bite of food. *"I had forgotten how good food is,"* she said. *"And to drink water is kind of indescribable. I have missed it so much."* She took a drink and sighed. She wiped her hand across her lips. *"I see you have many questions."*

I nodded again.

"But first I have one of my own. Then I will tell you what you want to know."

"You can ask me anything," I said.

"Good. We are communicating well. My question is, can I borrow your jacket? This body is cold."

***

Pepkari sat next to me on the table wrapped up in my jacket that was too big for her. I realized she needed more, so while she was finishing her food I ran into the house.

Hilary was still watching TV. I ignored her and ran upstairs. I left a minute later with some of Hilary's clothes I had stuffed under my shirt.

Pepkari understood exactly how to put them on. I guess she knew from reading my thoughts. She pulled on a pair of jeans and a t-shirt easily and even tightened the belt, so they fit her well. The shirt was too long, and she rolled up the jeans so she wouldn't trip. She looked exactly like a girl playing dress-up in her mom's clothes.

I guess she took that thought from my mind as well, because she said, *"Well, if I look like a human child then I am one who is over one hundred and twenty thousand years old!"* She laughed and the sound was like her Neanderthal language. High and musical.

She turned her face to mine and looked into my eyes. She started to speak.

"Yes, I am what your people call a Neanderthal. You are correct. And this is no prank. I am real. I see in your mind that you know some of our history.

We developed our minds four hundred and fifty thousand years before we met you. We lived through cold times and hot times and we learnt to communicate with our thoughts.

When your people evolved, we knew that you were our cousins. You were taller than us and quicker. But your minds were not developed. You hunted and survived but you had no culture. No language. We wanted to help you. So, we taught you some of our ways.

We showed you how to paint and to use your mouths and bodies to make language. We showed you how the stones could be cut to make hunting easier. We taught you the secrets of fire. And you were quick learners. But still, your minds could not communicate with each other. So, there were things and ideas that you could not understand."

Pepkari stopped and drank some more water.

"But couldn't you teach us?" I asked.

"No. It's not something you can teach. If a bird doesn't have wings you cannot teach her to fly. But we hoped that in time, you would develop a brain that could... be flexible."

"So, what happened?"

"Evolution is a long and complex process. One species evolves one way to fit in and adapt with what is around them. Telepathy was not for your species. Although, I do see in your mind that your brains have changed. There is potential there. Maybe now, we could teach you."

"I would like that. If you could teach me."

"Maybe. But you are not asking the question I can see at the front of your mind. Why don't you ask me? You should ask, because sometimes the questions we have are so big we need to speak them."

I nodded. I think I understood what she meant. *"Ok then. I will ask you. What happened to you all? Why did you all die? What happened? Did we kill you? And how can you come back now? How can bones grow flesh? And how can…"*

"Stop!" she said. *"That's lots of questions. And if you keep talking your questions will become clearer than the answers."*

"Ok. I see." I didn't. But I wanted to hear more.

"You didn't kill us. What you call your species, humans, were violent. You killed each other sometimes and I see in your mind that you still do. But you didn't hurt us. You couldn't."

"So, where did you all go?"

"We left. We died."

"I don't understand."

"I know. I will try to explain. With our brains we are able to see into thoughts. We also discovered that we could separate our own thoughts from our bodies."

"You mean, your mind can leave your body and then just go back into it?"

"No," she laughed again. *"It's not like that. A body is a body. It is made of meat. The brain is also made from meat. But the mind – the thoughts that come from that brain – can live on their own. But when they leave the body, they cannot come back. The body, without thought, cannot take care of itself. It dies. It goes away. Then the mind cannot return."*

"I think I understand."

"Clever boy!"

I ignored the implied sarcasm. *"So, you all left your bodies and died. Why?"*

"We wanted to give you a chance to change and to evolve. We realized that we were taking something away from you."

"What?"

"We had evolved for hundreds of thousands of years on our own. We realized that even though we were trying to help you, we were interfering. You needed a chance to do things your own way. Some of our people thought that you might evolve in completely different ways to us. So, we decided to leave. To leave the world and let you do your own thing. We wanted to return someday. To come back to our home and meet you again. As friends. As equals."

"And that is what you are doing now? But I thought you said you couldn't return to your bodies."

"We couldn't. But this body you see now is a different body. We have learnt that we can control the tiny parts of matter that make things. You call the bits you know about atoms or molecules. We can concentrate our thoughts and pull these atoms together. To make new bodies. All things are made of the same stuff. Everything is basically mud. But it's how you put the mud together that makes it different."

"And now here you are." I sat back. This was so much to understand.

Pepkari put her hand on my shoulder.

"Yep. Here I am." She grinned. *"I know this is a lot to understand. But you are doing very well. Use some imagination and you'll be fine. You see now, I think we can be friends. I think you have a lot to teach me, as I have a lot to teach you."* Pepkari stopped. She looked down and frowned.

"But the others, the others like me, they are not so lucky. I can see them. We are connected. Now they are locked in little rooms and angry humans are asking them questions. They think we are dangerous. My people want to leave again. But, I…" she looked into my eyes, *"I have seen your mind. We can be friends. I see what you are."*

"I think we can be friends too," I said. Then I had a horrible thought. Hilary. She said she had called a friend in town.

"I'll be back in a minute," I said to Pepkari.

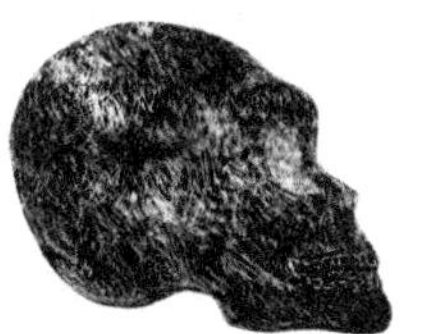

6

Human history

"Hilary! What did you tell your friend?"

Hilary was looking at her cell – flipping through text.

"What's it got to do with you?"

"You told her, didn't you?"

"Told her what?"

"You know what! I thought we had a plan."

"We did. But I've changed it. I called her and then I called the police. They're coming to see the bones. They said they would send a car to take a look. And if the bones are dangerous, they promised me a reward."

"You idiot!" I said. *"You don't know what you've done!"*

Hilary was angry too. *"You lied to me! The police told me that the bones are very, very dangerous. You lied!"*

"When did you call them?"

"They'll be here soon. I told them it was your idea!"

At that same moment, I heard them. Sirens. They were coming closer.

I grabbed my car keys and ran out. Pepkari had opened the barn door. She was standing by the car, her face upturned to the sun. Her hands spread out.

"Pepkari!" I yelled.

"I know," she said, and looked at me. *"We have to go. I don't want to be locked in a room. I want to keep talking to you."*

"Me too," I said and pulled open the car doors. We jumped in.

***

I looked in my mirror. Only one police car was following us. Its lights and sirens were on.

My heart was pounding. My foot was flat to the floor. I have never driven so fast. I couldn't let them get hold of Pepkari. I understood what she had told me. Of course, the government had used the police and army to take away all the Neanderthal remains. When they'd studied them, they would have quickly realized what was happening. And now, all those Neanderthals would be in secret labs around the world being questioned. There was no way the government would believe them. They probably thought that aliens were invading or something.

I glanced at Pepkari. She was looking out of her window and smiling happily. She turned and caught my eye.

"I can see that you are worried Erwin, but isn't it all so fantastic? Do you see what an amazing world this is? It truly is the most amazing cradle. I have missed it so much! The trees, the grasses

and hills. Blue sky! Just look!" She rolled down the window and pointed up. I looked back in the mirror again.

"Stop the car and pull over!" A loud voice came from the police car. *"Pull over now or we will open fire."*

"That's rubbish," I said. I looked at Pepkari. *"You don't have to worry. Police don't have guns in England."*

Pepkari looked at me again and smiled. *"Actually, they're not lying."*

And then there was a crack and the back window exploded. I ducked my head as glass hit the back of my neck. I pulled at the wheel and the car drove off the road and through a fence. We bumped up and down into a field, but I kept the car straight. I looked in the mirror again. Behind me I saw the police car also pull off the road, but they hit a bump and rolled over. The car landed on its roof. There were no other cars in sight. I kept driving across the field. I crashed through another fence and then we were on a little dirt road.

"That was close!" I said. My voice was shaking. I turned to smile at Pepkari. But she was not smiling. She was pushing her hand into her shoulder. There was blood coming from between her fingers. Her face was whiter than usual.

"Something stung me," she said quietly. *"Maybe a bee or a wasp."*

And then her eyes closed, and she fell forward.

***

Pepkari was alive but unconscious. I stopped the car and using my t-shirt I tied a bandage tight around the top of her arm to stop the blood. I kept driving until I saw another barn. I pulled her out and quickly carried her in. The barn was empty. I put her down using my jacket as a pillow. I wiped my hand across my face to clear the blood and tears from my eyes. I had to do something. She couldn't die!

***

Pepkari's eyes opened when I dug into her arm with a small knife from my field kit bag.

"Thank you," she said.

"What for?"

"For stopping the bleeding and for helping me. The police behind us were ok. They were unhurt."

"I don't care about them!" I said, wiping my hand over my eyes again. *"They tried to kill you."*

"They were just doing as they were instructed. They are not bad people."

"They tried to kill us!" I couldn't stop the tears.

"Hey!" she said. *"It's ok. Don't worry. We are safe now."*

I felt like a child, protected from a scary dog by its mother.

"Yes, but for how long?" I took a deep breath. *"But never mind. We can worry about that later. First, we need to do this. It's going to hurt."*

"I know. You need to get the bullet out of my arm. Go ahead. It's ok."

I dug the knife in. Pepkari's expression didn't change. Her eyes remained fixed to mine. She was smiling again.

"I said go ahead. I can stop the pain. Just take it out and I can start to fix myself."

I pushed until the knife hit metal. I felt sick. I dug and then using tweezers from my bag, I pulled out the bullet. I dropped it to the floor.

"Good," Pepkari said. She closed her eyes. *"Now I need to rest and fix the wound. You just relax. Play a game or something."*

"There's no connection here," I said. But Pepkari didn't answer.

***

An hour passed. Then another. I just sat and looked at her.

Here I was in another barn, looking at a one hundred-thousand-year-old woman repair her body from a bullet that the police had fired at us. I have never even been stopped by the police before! I have never run from the law!

I started to panic. What was going to happen now? I couldn't go back to my old job. And now that the police knew about Pepkari and me they would never stop chasing us. Hilary had said the army was involved. I was a thirty-two-year-old history professor on the run from the police and the army for hiding a Neanderthal woman. What was I going to do?

And then I looked at Pepkari's face and nothing else mattered. My job, my life… were nothing, compared to this. I was looking at the beginning of all human history. The origins of thought and human life. And she had told me that life was much more than I could possibly have imagined. What was one life… my life… compared to that?

She opened her eyes and smiled again.

"There. All finished." She patted her arm.

The hole was completely gone.

"Good as new," she said and smiled even wider. *"But now I'm hungry again."*

7

Our playground

We drove on for another fifty or so miles. I wanted to get as far away as possible.

I stopped off at a gas station and bought us some junk food. Pepkari freaked out over the chocolate.

"I saw the word in your head, but I never realized it was like this?"

"It's just a Mars Bar!" I laughed as she tried to fit another whole bar into her mouth.

I pulled off at a little motel and checked in. Pepkari kept my jacket on to hide the bloodstain on her shirt. We parked and scurried into the room. It was evening time. I was exhausted. Pepkari looked wide awake.

The room had twin beds. I lay down and pulled the sheets over me. Pepkari did the same in her bed.

"You need to sleep," she said from across the room. She was lying on her side, her hands tucked under her cheek. I turned on to my side facing her and looked back.

"I know," I said.

"But you want to know more. Such curiosity! It's something your people and mine share. We want to know everything." She laughed and again the beautiful sound was like music in my ears. *"I guess it's something all life shares,"* she said. Her eyes danced. *"So, ask me, then. You know you want to."*

It felt like she was teasing me.

I took a breath. I felt warm and sleepy. But she was right. I had to know more.

"What was it like? You and your people left your bodies thousands of years ago and you've been traveling. Where? Where did you go? What did you see?"

"We went…" she said, *"…everywhere."* She turned her eyes and looked up.

And then she filled my head with the universe as she continued to speak.

"Without our bodies there was nowhere we couldn't go. The whole galaxy became our playground. At first, we stayed close to home. We explored the other planets in the solar system. Planets you call Mars, Jupiter, Saturn. And then we looked outwards and we moved away. Some of us traveled together, others went in groups. I traveled alone. I have always been someone who likes my own time. I left the solar system and traveled out. I wish I could show you."

She smiled at me again. *"You would love it, Erwin! I danced through sparkles of light as they bounced from ancient ice seas on far away worlds, a thousand times as big as Earth. I rushed into black holes and pushed my mind into other times and other places. I watched as a star was born – its energy and light flowing over me like…"* she paused, trying to find the words, *"… like the best chocolate ever!"*

"But how could you feel if you were just… mind?"

"Mind can feel – just not in the same way as flesh. And sometimes we grew flesh to explore planets and cultures physically. We would reach into the earth, as we did here, and simply create new bodies to exist within."

"Cultures? You met others? Other life?"

"Yes, we did. There were planets with life that moved slowly, as big as a mountain. And planets where the life was so small that one tiny puddle contained whole civilizations. I rolled with a gas being who filled an entire planet and danced with giant winged beings who live in cities made of ice crystals. And I met others like me."

"Other Neanderthals?"

"No. But other minds that were traveling. At first, I didn't know what they were. I could just feel something thinking close to me. But when I learned to open my mind further, I realized what they were. Other travelers. Other explorers who had learnt to free themselves."

I had to interrupt. *"It's so strange. The idea that a mind can be freed from a brain. It just doesn't make sense. How is that possible?"*

Pepkari took a deep breath.

"OK – buckle up kid – I'm about to rock your world!"

That made me laugh out loud.

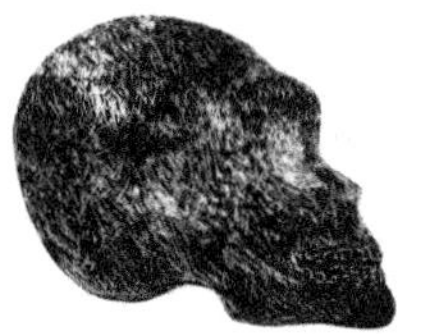

8

Prism light

"Seriously though, I can only find about half the words I need in your head. So, this is going to be tough. But let's give it a go."

Pepkari pushed herself up and sat on the edge of her bed. Her feet swinging over the edge. She drummed her fingers on her knee.

"The brain is a machine. A good machine, but a machine. It's like a prism. And your mind is like light. Sort of. Oh wow, this is hard." She chuckled.

"Try," I pressed.

"But your brain is more than that. It also creates mind. You have the word entanglement in your brain, but you don't seem to understand it very well."

"It's something to do with science, right?"

"Yes. When tiny stuff is smashed together in certain ways it becomes entangled. It becomes connected to each other. The mind is trillions of bits of stuff that you don't have a name for yet – or maybe you do, I'm not sure."

"What do you mean?"

"Well, you've sort of heard about dark energy and that might be it. Look, there are particles of stuff out there, kind of like mind atoms. You can't see them yet, because they don't really interact much with this time-space. They have no electrical charge and no real mass. And these mind atoms are everywhere."

"Where do they come from?"

"Well, when universes kind of rub together they make baby universes that appear in a massive explosion that carves out all new scientific laws and stuff. You call it the Big Bang, right?"

"Yes. But where is the baby universe?"

"You're in it. It's this one. Universes make babies like a lot of living things. They rub together, mix bits of each other and out pops a new one. Elegant and effective. Some of the universes that are born don't have the right laws to make life – and some do. Look, we are getting off the point a bit."

"Sorry, it's all so… weird." I had to get my head around the fact that in a few sentences Pepkari has revealed the origins of the cosmos.

"That ain't the half of it."

"Go on."

"So, in the Big Bang, all this stuff is made. All the bits to make the universe you can see and all the bits you can't see. The stuff you can't see is actually the building blocks of mind. Mind atoms. Let's call them cognitons."

"What?"

"Hey, I thought that was clever. Kind of like electrons but with a bit of cognitio in front. Means to think in Latin."

"I know."

"Well... duh. How do you think I know?"

"Good point. So, everything has a mind? Is that what you are saying?"

"No, I didn't say that. Everything has cognitons inside, yes. Apples, stars, nebulae, coke... even chocolate. But it's only when you get trillions of cognitons connected – entangled - that they become mind. Mind like yours. Mind like mine. And all the other flavors of mind out there."

"And how does that happen?"

"Right. We are getting there. It's the brain. Or something like it anyway. The brain is a smashing machine. It fires electrons into each other. And the cognitons kind of hitch a ride on the electrons. And, as the brain grows and time passes, more and more cognitons are smashed onto each other. As they smash, they become entangled. And that entangled stuff is what we call mind. The cognitons are entangled, and when the brain rots away, the entangled cognitons – the mind – is free to go and wander.

The brain is incredible. It takes different forms on different cradles – sometimes it's just a massive electrical storm, but basically, if the universe has the right laws, it finds a way to smash the bits together."

"Like the LHC?" I interrupted with a rare insight. *"The Large Hadron Collider?"*

"Exactly!" Pepkari clapped her hands. *"Nailed it! The brain is like a highly efficient miniature LHC: fine-tuned to create mind from cognitons. It's how cognitons can interact with this level of reality.*

Without the brain to smash things together, cognitons just kind of float around, not really dealing with the whole time-space thing."

"How so?"

"Well, think of dreams. Time is weird, right?"

"Yes."

"That's your mind showing its nature. Thought doesn't come from the electricity, it's from the other stuff. And that other stuff has a different relationship with time. The electricity in the brain helps create the entangled mind and then also carry out its wishes. So, when mind says jump, the brain jumps. It's a tool."

"But you said the brain was a prism?"

"Right. It's a bit clumsy, but I stand by it." Pepkari paused and swung her feet again. *"Or sit by it."* She grinned.

"So light is all around us, right? But you really see it when it goes through a prism. I'm saying if the mind is like light, then the brain is like a prism. The prism refracts the light. That's also kind of what the brain does for the mind. It allows us to see it."

"Well, it feels like my prism is cracking!" I laughed at my own wit.

"Oh, don't joke about that. It happens," said Pepkari. *"Sometimes the brain forms wrongly or maybe accidents or old age damage it. Then the light can't get out properly. The mind is still in there – it just looks wrong when it shines out."*

"I think I understand…" I said slowly. *"Alzheimer's, mental illness…"*

"Well, there's more to it. But fundamentally, yes. The good news is, when it leaves the brain, it's not fractured anymore. So, the problem goes away."

I closed my eyes; my thoughts leaping about like fleas on a hot roof.

9

Prism light

"And you've met other minds with no brains. Just floating around in space." I sighed again and massaged the bridge of my nose. *"Alien life from other worlds… it's… unbelievable."*

"Some from other worlds, some much closer to home."

"What do you mean?" I pushed myself up. *"Mars? Did you meet Martians?"*

Pepkari laughed. *"Little green men with ray guns? No. The planet you call Mars has never had much luck with life."*

I was confused. *"But, where then?"*

"Come on Erwin. Use your imagination. I know there's a spark of intelligence in there somewhere."

I frowned but relaxed when I saw her eyes glint with what I was beginning to understand was a wicked sense of humor.

"Venus?" I suggested.

Pepkari sighed theatrically and then said,

"Erwin, which planet orbiting this star do you know with a proven track record of creating and nurturing life?"

Now it was my turn to sigh. *"Pepkari, you seem to think we are more advanced than we are. We've been to the moon and we've sent machines to Mars and a couple of the other planets, but that's about it – the only planet we know anything about is…."*

And then understanding flowed through my mind as a rain swollen stream – *"You're talking about Earth! This planet!"*

Pepkari clapped laconically and laughed, *"Take a bow Erwin, you've officially become the most informed of your species."*

My mind was turning over too quickly – jumping from idea to idea – racing.

"You met dinosaurs out there? Space dinosaurs?" My voice was too high and beginning to crack.

Pepkari shushed me and made calming motions with her hands.

"Is this all a bit too much?" she asked with concern. *"Your thoughts are all over the place. You want to take a break?"*

"No!" I nearly yelled. *"Sorry,"* I said quieter. I took a breath and let it out slowly. *"I'm ok. Please, I'm just trying to understand. I really want to."*

"Ok. But lie back down and try and relax. Slow your heart. Slow your mind. Then I'll try."

I put my head onto the crook of my arm and lay, my eyes fixed and softened by the dark green eyes of this being, so like, yet so unlike myself.

"Good," she said quietly and then, in the same steady voice she continued.

"We weren't the first and you won't be the last. It took us about half a million years to develop from our first conscious thoughts to a spacefaring race. Your species is already reaching out away from the cradle and…"

"The cradle?" I interrupted. *"You said that before, in the car. What do you mean?"*

"It's our name for this planet. This is our home cradle planet. There are other cradles out there, planets that seem to be perfect for producing and nurturing life. Not so many, but enough. And the pattern seems the same. Life emerges. Sometimes the seeds for life are carried between planets on asteroids and comets and other times it seems to spontaneously emerge from chemical soups, pulled and pushed by heat and climate. It takes a billion years or so for it to form into complex beings and then the magic of mind happens. Once a species takes a first thought or picks up an object to use for something else then the rest seems to be inevitable. In half a million years or so, they develop and reach the stars — sometimes in machines they build or sometimes just with mind, like us. Each journey is different, each species takes their own path, and each develops its own unique beauty and form. It's stunning actually."

Pepkari paused for a moment and in that fraction of time I saw it through her eyes. A species as a baby bird, leaving the egg, growing and then taking its first steps and flight. Flying from the nest that can be used again by a new generation.

And us, humanity, just beginning on our own tentative path: the moon, Mars and beyond. It took us just thirty thousand years from chipping at flint stones to building machines that could leave the solar system. Who knows where we will be in another thirty thousand? And if we had half a million years to develop like Pepkari's people, what could we achieve?

Pepkari had started to speak again.

"So, you can do the math. In less than a million years, my people and your people both developed to this point. This planet has been producing complex life for nearly half a billion years. So yes, we weren't the first. And you won't be the last."

The scientist in me was not satisfied. *"But the geological record? Fossils? Remains? If there had been such complex life – such sophistication – where is the evidence?"*

Pepkari laughed softly. *"Early on, we asked the same questions. But it's simple really. It's a question of duty. When you reach a certain level of development you start to realize your responsibility as temporary caretakers of the cradle. You see the other species emerging and when it's time for you to fly the nest,"* – I guess she had seen the analogy in my mind – *"you clean it up. You don't want the new species getting all messed up with feelings of inferiority – everybody needs the confidence to move forward. And what you miss, time takes care of the rest."*

"But buildings, energy sources… all the things a species needs to reach space. Surely some of that would survive?"

Pepkari tutted.

"You're still not using your imagination. Even now, your species is trying to build in ways that leave as little impact as possible on the cradle. In a thousand years or so, you'll be taking energy from places you cannot yet understand. The further along the journey a species takes, the less its impact on the cradle is felt and the greater the sense of responsibility. You realize you are part of something much bigger and you do what you can to protect that. To give something back. We made the same mistakes as you - early on; materials that polluted and wouldn't erode, fuel that irradiated. But, in under a thousand years or so, we worked out how to clean it all up. We learnt to build

with living matter, and we learnt to power with starlight and dark space. And as I say, half a million years is long enough for any traces you miss to be worn away."

I thought of the oldest human buildings – maybe twelve thousand years old – there would be no trace in another ten thousand.

I nodded. *"I think I understand. But you could have helped us. We've had a hard time. War, pain, disease…"*

"No, we all have to learn for ourselves. The hard things. We're all builders, Erwin. Life. I don't mean houses – I mean civilizations. Cultures. Understanding. Sometimes pain can help build something. Love builds better things. But, in a way, all of it… I mean the good stuff and the bad – it all builds. Even destruction can build."

I thought of the rain forests where devastating fires cleared ground and provided nutrients for new life to grow. I think I understood. A little bit anyway.

And Pepkari talked of other beings and worlds. She spoke of the vastness of space and the jewels that were the cradles. She sang me songs from distant cultures and described the gentle caress of a solar storm.

The pictures from her words were pulling me out. But sleep was beginning to take me – pulling me in.

"I want to do that," I said, my voice heavy with exhaustion. *"I want to see that."*

"And I can show you," were the last words I heard.

10

Hunted

"Erwin, wake up. Your people are coming."

Pepkari was standing over me. I sat up.

Pepkari said, *"The hotel receptionist. She recognized you from a news report. You are hunted. We are hunted. What do you want to do?"*

I pulled on my clothes. *"I don't want them to catch you Pepkari. I want to go."*

"Ok. Then we go," she said simply.

As our car screeched out from the motel, I saw a line of cars speeding our way – police cars and army vehicles.

"They're faster than us," I said. *"We have to make a run for it. On foot."*

I pulled the car over and jumped out. I took Pepkari's hand and we ran into the trees. I heard dogs barking and the sounds of many people following us.

"It's our only chance," I said.

We ran for two or three minutes. But Pepkari's legs were smaller than mine and the sounds of those following came always closer.

There was a cottage in front of us. There were no lights on.

"Maybe the people in there can help us," I said. But I knew there was no hope. I just had to keep trying. To save her. To save myself.

I pushed at the door. It swung open. The house was not used. There was no light and spiders' webs everywhere. I slammed the door shut behind me and looked for something to drag in front of it. I pushed an old piano with no keys into place. I knew it was pointless, but I couldn't stop.

Pepkari just stood in the middle of the room and looked at me. She sat down. She patted the floor with her hand.

"Come on Erwin. Come and sit next to me. Let's be together. I don't think we have much time."

Lights were shining through the trees and I could see people moving outside. It was over. I knew it. And I felt all my energy leave me. I was defeated.

I sat down by her. She put her big head on my shoulder. She let out a sigh. She put her hand over mine. My fist was clenched. She wound her fingers into my palm. Relaxing my hand.

"Erwin," she said quietly. *"I have loved getting to know you and I want to know you more."*

"Me too," I said, and felt like a teenager on his first date.

"But the others, my people, they have gone already."

"What do you mean? Have they escaped?"

Pepkari laughed.

"Not like you are thinking, no. But they have left. We have been communicating with each other and they think that your people are not ready to have us back yet. You see, your governments have asked us questions. They have even tried to experiment on our bodies. You know we don't have to feel pain. But this shows us that humans need more time. Maybe in another few thousand years humans will be ready to accept what is so different. But now, you guys need more time to evolve on your own. It's a shame, but there it is." She sighed again.

A loudspeaker crackled outside. A man's voice said. *"Dr Erwin Katz. We know you are in there. And we know who you are with. You must come out and give the alien terrorist to us. Immediately. If not, we will come in by force. You have two minutes."*

Pepkari pushed herself up. *"But you can come too. I can show you how. We can travel together for a thousand years. Then when we come back, you can help us talk to your people. Would you like to?"*

I thought. I thought about my parents, my friends. I thought about my work. My university. I thought about my garden and cups of tea. Pepkari looked at me. Her eyes were kind. They were full of water.

"I see," she said. *"Not yet. You need time."* She smiled and then leant forward and kissed me gently on the cheek. *"I'm going to miss you Erwin."*

And then she closed her eyes and put her big heavy head back on my lap. She sighed once more, and then was still.

II

The Beginning

The army took Pepkari's body away.

I was held in prison for a month – solitary. The times I was alone I thought of Pepkari – her eyes, her smile. And when the thoughts of her turned to ache, I went over and over all that I had learnt.

When I thought of those first days – the bodies rising from the mud, I imagined them on countless other worlds. The bodies forming, under the stars and then a breath is taken, eyes open, and see.

And when I wasn't alone, my captors asked me all kinds of questions. And then they asked them a thousand times more. I told them the truth, but they didn't believe me. They couldn't believe me. And then, they let me go. I guess that since all the Neanderthals were dead, they weren't so worried anymore.

But the press knew. Someone from the army prison or maybe Hilary, I don't know, had told them that I had protected one of the alien terrorists. That was what the Neanderthals were called now. Alien terrorists. If it weren't so stupid, it would be funny. I'm sure Pepkari would have found it hilarious.

My university wouldn't even return my calls. My parents stopped talking to me and my friends looked the other way when they saw me.

I moved. I left town and moved up north. I got a job serving beer in a little pub. It was fine for a week until one of the customers recognized me. I was sacked. I moved again and then again. But wherever I went, it was the same story. Someone recognized me and I started again.

A week ago, I arrived here. A tiny fishing village in the North of Scotland. Nobody knew me until this morning. And then…

***

I was working in a coffee shop, serving strong black coffee to the fisherman when a woman walked in. She was tall with long black hair. She looked out of place – like a businesswoman or high-powered lawyer. She wore an Armani suit, and her hair was pinned up over her high cheekbones and almond eyes. I gave her another look. She could have been a model. My boss was washing glasses. He was looking at her too. She sat down at a table in the corner and looked at the menu. I walked over.

"What can I get you?" I asked.

"What's good?" she said.

"Not much," I said. *"Coffee's ok. I guess."*

"Do you have any chocolate?" she said. *"You know how I love chocolate."*

I looked at her. I didn't recognize her. *"I'm sorry,"* I said. *"Do I know you?"*

"Yes. And I know you Dr Erwin Katz. Student of Neanderthals."

"I think you have me confused with someone else." Damn it! She must be a journalist.

And then she looked at me.

Different eyes. But the same.

Different lips. Same smile.

"Pepkari!" But how can you… how can it be you?"

"Oh, come on, Erwin! You know we can control atoms to create bodies. Don't you think we can make any body we want? It's just stuff after all! Use some imagination!" She grinned at me.

I grinned back. I sat down opposite her. She took my hands. I could see my boss scowling at me. I ignored him.

"So, you're back," I said. My heart was racing.

"For now. Not for long. Some of us are going to stay and watch humans to see how long it takes them to grow up a bit. But me, I have a hunger for travel. There's a whole new galaxy I've been wanting to visit for oh…" she frowned, *"…the last five thousand years or so. I just thought I'd pop in and see if you've changed your mind."*

She looked at me. She looked into my eyes and behind them, into my thoughts.

"So, how about it? What do you say? You want to come traveling?"

"I think you know my answer," I said. I wanted to jump up and down and shout and laugh.

"Yes, I think I do. But some things are better said out loud." Her bright eyes crinkled into a grin.

I nodded. I turned to look at my boss.

"Hey!" I said. *"Boss!"*

He put down a glass and glared at me. *"What?"*

"I quit."

The end.

Andy Coombs   Sarah Scho

Viking Kite stories are written by Swedish-English writers, Andy Coombs and Sarah Scho - both authors and teachers with more than 50 books published and a million books sold in Sweden. Their work and stories have been read and loved by young Swedish minds for more than twenty years and in 2021 are available in translation internationally.

Andy and Sarah live just outside Stockholm in a blue wooden house next to a forest. They live with their tiny black and white dog, Nimly.

Viking Kite stories celebrate life with fun and imagination, encouraging young readers of all ages to see things in new ways.

"Everyone gets to fly the kite."